DEER *in the* HOLLOW

Efner Tudor Holmes
ILLUSTRATED BY
Marlowe deChristopher

PHILOMEL BOOKS
NEW YORK

Published by Philomel Books, a division of The Putnam & Grosset Group,

200 Madison Avenue, New York, NY 10016. Published simultaneously in Canada.

Printed in Hong Kong by South China Printing Co. (1988) Ltd.

Lettering by David Gatti. The text is set in Bembo.

The pictures for *Deer in the Hollow* were executed on canvas in alkyd oil paints

and regular oils, with a combination of direct painting, glazing, and scumbling.

Library of Congress Cataloging-in-Publication Data

Holmes, Efner Tudor. Deer in the hollow /

Efner Tudor Homes; illustrated by Marlowe deChristopher. p. cm.

Summary: A young boy's special relationship with the forest animals culminates

on the day before Christmas when the animals are able to repay his care.

[1. Forest animals—Fiction. 2. Animals—Fiction. 3. Christmas—Fiction.]

I. deChristopher, Marlowe, ill. II. Title. PZ7.H735De 1993

[Fic]—dc19 88-29322 CIP AC ISBN 0-399-21735-5

1 3 5 7 9 10 8 6 4 2

First Impression

For Judy and Bill Egan

ETH

"Sometimes our inner light goes out, but it is blown again into flame by an encounter with another human being. Each of us owes the deepest thanks to those who have rekindled this inner light."

ALBERT SCHWEITZER

For my parents

MdeC

In the far north country of New England, a small village lay at the foot of a steep hillside. The villagers lived in close friendship with each other. When Seth came to live with his grandfather and grandmother, the people asked no questions and welcomed the boy into their lives.

Seth was a quiet child, rarely speaking to those around him. He preferred to spend his time on the hillside roaming the woods. Some of the villagers said they had seen the boy in the winter woods with birds eating seeds from his hands. Seth often brought home baby birds and squirrels that had fallen from their nests, caring for them until they could return to the forest. He knew where the deer huddled for shelter in the winter and where a mother fox made her den.

Sometimes the villagers talked among themselves about Seth. They worried about the child often wandering alone in the woods. But Seth knew nothing of that. He never feared the forest that smelled of warm earth and of ferns growing in shady hollows among moss-covered rocks always damp and cool.

Once when Seth stayed in the woods too long, his grandfather went to look for him. He found the boy sitting on a stump. A doe and her fawn were nearby eating some apples Seth had given to them. Several other deer were nearby nibbling at the bushes. Occasionally the doe would lift her head and gaze calmly at the boy. But when the old man came in sight, the deer bounded away. Seth's grandfather smiled. It was as if Seth really could talk to the animals as he had wanted to when he was younger and his grandmother told him all the animals talked at midnight on Christmas Eve.

That year winter came early, with great storms, and the snow lay heavy and deep in the silent woods. Now Seth went to the forest every day, traveling far up the hillside, his snowshoes packing little trails where he scattered seeds for the birds and squirrels and apples and

carrots for the deer. He worried most about the deer, knowing the deep snow buried much of their food. His grandmother fretted he would catch cold from being out so long. Seth paid little attention.

But the daily trips in the wind and cold took their toll. Just before Christmas, Seth became very ill. For days he ran a high fever and hardly recognized his grandfather and grandmother when they came to sit with him. Outside the wind blew constantly and the thermometer dropped below zero. Seth's grandmother had to scrape the frost off the window so Seth could look out and see the hillside.

The day before Christmas, Seth's fever broke. He sat downstairs by the fireplace, wrapped in his quilt, and politely smiled at the neighbors who came to wish him Merry Christmas. But his thoughts were up on the hill with the deer and other animals trying to find food.

Seth felt restless and his grandmother made him go to bed early. But Seth couldn't sleep. Finally he got up and stood by the window looking onto the field that stretched from the house to the foot of the hill.

As Seth stood there something caught his eye. It was two deer, a doe and her fawn, running across the snow. Occasionally their feet would break through the crust. Suddenly another dark figure came onto the field, running fast and low to the ground. Seth knew it was

a dog, and he knew the deer could not run away fast enough. Without thinking, Seth scrambled into some clothes. He pulled on a heavy sweater and, opening his window, he quietly climbed out.

The night was cold and clear, with the stars brilliant in the sky and the air smelling of wet snow. Far up the hillside Seth could hear the dog barking. He knew then the deer were still leading the chase. He began to run and the cold air hurt his lungs. He no longer heard the dog barking, only the sound of his feet thudding against the snow.

As he started up the hill, he realized how foolish he had been. Already his feet were cold and he felt weak and dizzy. But he did not turn back for the ugly thought of the dog attacking the helpless and terrified deer floundering in the snow drove him on.

He came to a ledge and stood for a moment trying to catch his breath. There below him he saw the two deer turning and facing the dog weakly in a last attempt to save themselves.

Seth yelled at the dog and grabbed a stick that was pointing through the snow. But the stick was frozen into the ground. Seth tugged at it frantically. As he did, a wave of dizziness overcame him and he fell from the ledge.

Far into the night Seth's grandmother woke uneasily. The house was unusually cold. She got up to put another blanket on Seth. She stood at the door of his empty room, staring through the open window at the hillside dark in the moonlight. Then she turned and ran to get her husband.

Minutes later the field was full of men, their lights bobbing in the dark. They walked in silence through the night as they followed Seth's

grandfather to the hill. But they slowed as they reached the bottom of the hill. The wind had begun to erase the tracks.

Now it is said that as the men began climbing the hill, a doe and her half-grown fawn appeared. She showed no fear of the men but turned and began walking deep into the woods. Silently the men followed until they came to a part of the woods where great beech trees and ledges formed a hollow.

Moonlight fell through the naked branches onto the snow where the boy lay. Around him in a great circle stood the creatures of the

forest standing at peace with one another. The forest was silent except for the birds singing in the trees above. They sang as if it were dawn.

When the procession of men led by the two deer appeared, the animals turned and vanished into the woods. The doe and her fawn came to Seth and stood for a moment.

One might say the men, cold and tired, had imagined all this. But there was the old grandfather kneeling in the snow, his head bowed, hugging his grandson.

Seth did not speak, but he smiled as he watched the two deer following the multitude of tracks on the snow leading into the forest.